STR   ⎯⎯⎯⎯⎯⎯⎯⎯⎯ ⎯⎯⎯VIS

STREET OF DREAMS

and other stories

Love and best weshes
Betty Lane 10/1/16

BETTY LANE

ISBN: 099291812X
ISBN 13: 9780992918125

STREET OF DREAMS

1

STREET OF DREAMS

THE WHIRR OF the dryer spun in and out of her con-
sciousness. When she moved her head the metal roll-
ers clacked on the inner side of the cover. She was trapped,
trapped in the gilded mirror in front of her. Her hair was
drawn into a coif, lending her a nun-like austerity. She
brooded over the fine red veins drawn by the hot air over
her nose and cheeks. Would they fade by the evening?

She could not concentrate on the so helpful shiny
magazines. Her hands flicked over the pages. The strands
of hair were being unrolled. Should she have tried this
new style today? She could imagine Roger's scathing re-
marks. All the pins were being removed; her hair was
being combed into unfamiliar shapes. What was happening to her, she thought above the hairdresser's patter.
With all of life to be lived, with momentous events taking place in the world, she was reduced to panic because
her hair-style might be a failure.

She arrived home before Roger. She surveyed the hall and living room. Magnolia paintwork and gleaming woodwork reassured her. It was immaculate. Yet there was a chance that an ashtray had been left full and forgotten, or yesterday's papers left on the rack. She moved a limp rose from the silver bowl. The roses were so lovely; they were reflected in the waxed table-top. The rose was too beautiful to be thrown away. It was no more faded and tired than she was. She moved from room to room. In the kitchen she anxiously nibbled some biscuits. Roger's key in the door startled her. She had not heard his car along the drive.

He was perfectly dressed as always. His dark city suit was dust free, his trousers sharp. His white shirt gleamed.

"What have they done to you?" He gave her a quick kiss.

"It's a mistake, I know. He wanted to try out a new style. I thought I would chance it."

"Take a chance, tonight! You haven't forgotten where we're going I suppose?"

"I haven't forgotten," said Stephanie. Dinner with the Carsons. She had been dreading it all day.

She followed him into the open-plan kitchen. The main cooker-switch had been left on. She saw it a moment before he did. He pressed the lever up: it clacked disapprovingly.

"You could burn the place down."

I didn't burn my flat down, she thought. She had a picture in her mind of its carefree cosiness. I've managed until now without burning any place down. But she said nothing. He rinsed out a milk bottle.

"You'll splash your suit."

"Somebody's got to keep things in order." Then, he started sifting through papers from his briefcase. She made tea in a silver teapot, and they ate thin sandwiches prepared by the morning help and left on the trolley. He stirred the pot with one hand and corrected the typed sheets with the other. She felt he was only playing at being busy. Surely there was no need to bring work home. And yet he was paid well enough, and advancing steadily.

She took another sandwich. She needed some sort of base for the hard drinking that there would be before dinner. She stirred her tea. "I met Stella when I was shopping this morning, and she asked us to drop in over the weekend. It would be lovely to have a quiet evening over in their garden. As we haven't got anything fixed, do you think ---"

"Waste of time, my girl."

"They are our only real friends, they're nice people."

"Nice people," he repeated. "We haven't much time for nice people, at least I haven't. If you've time for yack-yacketting while I'm up to my eyes in work, that's your affair. Now the Carsons may not be what you'd call nice. Just because he doesn't know who your precious Picasso is, you think he's a nobody, but I can tell you that man's

— 3 —

pretty smart." He picked up the typed sheet he had finished correcting and waved it at her. It crackled.

"He's going places, and just you watch how his old
lady backs him up. You could learn a thing or two. And
there's grooming for you. She's got natural good taste
and know-how. With those legs of hers."

Stephanie breathed deeply. She considered Bette's
style vulgar, her make-up overstated. You wouldn't think
so much of her if you saw her first thing before she's fixed
her face, she thought. And she'd be a bitch to live with.
But she said nothing. She needed all her energy to fix her
own disguise. She would need her wits to counter the
subtle social battle she knew the evening would become.
She would sit in an ostentatious room eating over-rich
food, making polite conversation. A successful outcome
would be a contract in the hand for Roger; more work
meant that she would see even less of him. And she would
be expected to offer a return invitation.

She longed to slip on her jeans and pullover, and run
over to Stella's. But she walked slowly up the stairs to
check that her brocaded dress was laid out on the quilted
bedspread, and to run a bath.

Now, she sat in a half-dream looking through the rain
spotted car window. She was lulled by the monotonous
flick-flap of the wipers as they drew raindrops over the
glass in a half-circle, not quite complete on her side. With
the mist formed by her breath and Roger's, the desolate
pavements were softened and blurred.

Gradually the ambience changed. The single houses with tree-lined drives became semi-detached with neat hedges; then they drove through streets of terraced houses with bare railings. Now, there were gaps in the railings and flattened areas overgrown with weeds and buddleia bushes. They were approaching the fringes of the town, with dilapidated houses and boarded up shops that marked the end of the old road. It had been overtaken by the new motorway. Down one of these mean streets was the room over a garage where Roger had lived when she first knew him.

Roger liked to use this garage for petrol. He said the prices were keener than motorway prices, and it offered good old- fashioned service. She thought also that it helped to remind him of the status he had achieved.

Roger drew in firmly and deftly onto the garage forecourt. He switched off the engine with precision, and put his pipe on the shelf.

"Put your window down, there's a good girl."

And before she could carry out his instructions, "Hurry up, I have to do everything. All you do is sit there dreaming. And your hair is terrible."

As she wound down the window, the soft fine rain fell on her hand. "Fill her up," he called over to the assistant. He spoke with an air of authority. Who was he acting for - an overworked garage hand?

She looked in the rain-spotted side mirror at her hair. Her image was blotted out drop by drop by the rain.

"Oil and water, sir?"

He understood the needs of the car, she thought, better than her own. "She could take a pint I would say."

Now he was walking round the car, looking carefully at the tyres. He drew in a deep breath as he surveyed the offside rear wheel. "Thought the steering was a bit strange," he said.

"Fit your spare, sir?"

"Right. But I'll be glad to have this one repaired now if you don't mind. Can't chance the motorway without a serviceable spare." He was showing notes from his wallet.

"Certainly sir. We can do it while you wait."

Roger leaned on the car bonnet. "Look, why don't you go into the office where it's quieter and phone the Carsons, there's a good girl. Tell them we'll be a bit late."

As she entered the garage shop, she noticed a card against the pane of a first floor window. 'Room to let.' It was in the window of Roger's old room. Their room was to let.

She phoned the Carsons quickly. Then she said to the woman behind the counter, a new unknown face, "You have a room to let. Can I see it?"

"I can't show it to you now," she said, "No-one to leave in the shop. Look, take the key, would you mind? It's very small though, hardly suit you." She looked hard at Stephanie.

Stephanie took the key quickly and went into the dim passage.

"Up the stairs to the top, then first on the left."

With her eyes closed she would have known. As the steps spiralled round, she heard the remembered creak from the loose board. Her gloved hand hesitated on the handle of the door. The bleached paint had lifted and flaked from the surface of the door leaving well-learned patterns of dark wood that spread like continents in her world of memory.

The room was little changed. The brass-knobbed bed still stood in the left-hand corner. Stripped now of bed-clothes, the mattress hollowed into the sagging springs. Although the window was open, she could smell gas from the badly fitting gas-ring, - 'cooking facilities' in the advertisement.

They had come upon the advert after days of room hunting. This was long before the car, before the money, before the business friends. There was no-one to impress in those days. Then it was only the need to find a room that Roger could afford, where he could work and sleep, and where she would be able to call each evening.

Even then they had been appalled when they first saw the room. The floor was covered in shiny linoleum. There was this cheerless bed, an ancient table, a book-case, a sagging shelf by the window, with a gas-ring and a washing-up bowl. Running water and a sink were on the floor below, next to the seat-less lavatory.

"There is a bit of a gas-leak," the landlady had said, "but we'll get it attended to. Until then, leave the window open."

How hard they had worked that first year. Every evening they would meet in this room after their work. He had been articled to an ageing solicitor in the town. As there had been no money for a premium, he worked for a very small salary. In the evening, an even harder job would begin. She had encouraged him to catch up on studies that should have been completed before leaving school: mathematics and English. If he passed in these subjects, he could begin to study for his first law exam. She had been glad to pay for the tutor he visited weekly.

She would arrive a little after him from her job in a hardware store, with groceries she bought in the lunch-hour. Somehow she would cook a meal. She would sit on the only chair, he would perch on the sagging bed. It had tasted good enough, better than the elaborate meals they sat down to these days.

Now, she walked over to the window and looked down over the forecourt. She could see their car, jacked up. The wheel had been taken for repair. She need not hurry.

She remembered some of the things he had said. She could hear his words. They echoed around the walls, "It's not just money I want for its own sake, but money means power. I don't want to be liked. Any fool can be liked. One must have the courage to have enemies; be feared and respected. Only then will you have power, be somebody."

"What do you want power for?" she had asked. But he had looked through her into his private dreams. "I don't want to be like my father, a pleb in a pleb's world, painting other people's houses all his life and dreaming of the business he would start if he had the capital or the luck. There's no such thing as luck, only hard work and being hard."

But she had been happy in those days. He had needed her so obviously. He was hopeless at looking after himself; this fact gave her a greater feeling of security than any assurance of love. Three evenings a week she would go to the local Art School. She needed to collect a portfolio of work to be accepted as a full-time student. But this dream was an amorphous one compared to Roger's clear-cut plans and ambitions, and in any case they needed her wages. Sometimes he would beg her to miss a class: he liked her to sit and read, or hear out his homework essays.

She moved the curtains back to check what was happening to the car. Roger was standing, feet apart, pipe in hand saying something to the man in overalls who knelt over the wheel. Still no need to hurry.

Her hands recoiled from the curtain fabric; the collected dust felt like sandpaper. She moved over to the cooking corner. Her fingers slipped over the edge of the chipped bowl. The familiar feel, and the faint smell of gas, awakened that place in her memory where one particular Sunday morning was preserved.

She had been away for a week on a painting course. It was their first week away from each other since they'd met. On Sunday morning she had risen early and walked the three miles from her home.

She had knocked on his door loudly to wake him. He opened the door at last, his face round and fresh with sleep. His pyjamas were rumpled. There was a tear along the seam through which she could see the thin, too white shoulder.

"I've missed you, it's been terrible," he had said, drawing her in and closing the door.

"I don't know how you managed without me," she had teased, looking carefully into his face. The muscles at the side of his mouth were clearly marked, and the flesh below the cheekbone drawn in. How beautiful he had been. Now that he was sleek and well-fed, the pads of flesh around chin and eye had softened and blurred. She had caressed his cheek. "You haven't been eating properly."

"If that's what you think, come and look at this little lot." The washing bowl was full of used dishes: they overflowed onto the table. Underneath was a week's collection of milk-bottles containing milk at different stages of fermentation, and a bin of rubbish. In a bowl beside them were piles of empty tins.

"You're utterly hopeless," she had said, secretly pleased.

She had moved towards the table. "It'll wait," he said. "Come, let me tell you what I've been doing."

He had lain back on the skimpy pillow, his head resting between the brass bars of the bedstead. She sat on the bed. He had taken her hand in his. She remembered again the rough-smooth feel of his hand, radiating warmth. The warmth had risen along her arm and into her body while they talked of the small happenings of the week.

He had released her hand for a moment to turn the knob of his radio. "Good concert this morning." The slow movement of Beethoven's seventh symphony enveloped them. Not a sound had come from outside their room; she felt as if there was nothing out there at all. No house, no garage, no street, no town: just a blue abyss in which they existed alone, timelessly.

He had tugged her hand, and she had taken off her shoes and her skirt and slipped in beside him. The sheets were grubby and she pointed this out to him without speaking. He made a wry face and smiled. It had mattered so little. There was the clean freshness of his body, luminous with warmth in the grey room. As he smiled, he showed the neat square teeth that had first endeared him to her, and pushed the muscles at the sides of his mouth into delicious fullness - 'podges' she had called them. There was always a moment in a relationship when one could say, ' I fell in love then,' - when the other said something in a particular voice, or moved in a particular way. She remembered the first time she had noticed his smile, how it had spread slowly to disclose his teeth, almost but not quite even. Yes, there it was, that slight unevenness, one tooth pressed a little too close to its pair, and set a shade behind. That was the very base of her love.

The music supported them languorously; within it were his slow caresses. He listened to the music with head turned away from her, touching her body idly, deliciously. The music had wrapped them together; when the last notes had died away, he had turned to her and buried his face in her breast: he had begun to make love with the lingering lack of haste of lovers who know each other well.

Looking up at the high ceiling with its ancient mouldings, they had dreamed and talked of the future. They had planned the details of the bedroom they would have when they could afford it. They planned their entire dream house, the garden, their friends, an entire day in their future life together. Then they got up at last and began the business of cleaning up. They carried all the milk bottles into the bath, put in the plug, and ran the water. They laughed delightedly when the bottles bobbed and spun in the rising water. He had gone downstairs to empty the bucket, and returned pale.

"It was alive with maggots," he had said. "Mm- mm-maggots," he said in mock horror, but she could see that he was really upset.

"Oh well, we all have to eat," she comforted him, and they laughed pointlessly and happily as they rinsed and polished and cleaned.

Now, Stephanie sat on the bed heavily. The hard metal frame was cold under her knees. She smoothed her hands over the bumps in the mattress. She looked up again at the ugly embossed ceiling where their dreams had been written. Then, we were happy, she thought. The happiest day of my life was in this small shabby room.

Now, our dreams have come true.

She stood up and straightened her skirt. She slipped on her fine leather gloves, opened the door, and went slowly down the stairs.

She handed the key back over the counter. "I knew it wouldn't suit you," the woman said.

It was bleak outside, still raining. Roger was standing now under the corrugated roof, watching the wheel nuts being tightened.

"You were a long time on the telephone. When you women get together, don't you yak. Can't seem to get a simple message through as men do."

"Well, you've only just finished."

"Into the car with you." He tipped the mechanic and got in beside her.

They made their way out to the old road, along the slip-road and on to the motorway before he spoke again. "I don't know where your mind is sometimes, you don't notice anything. Our old room was to let up there, and you didn't even give it a thought. Too busy gassing on the phone. We could have run up and taken a look at the old room for remembrance sake. Now you would never think of something like that. There's not much romance in you these days my girl. It's too late to go back now anyway."

"I suppose it is."

2

ANOTHER MILESTONE

I T WAS 1950--SOMETHING, and in those days we worried about how much travellers' currency allowance we would be able to take with us. Because of this limitation, Brits were known as the poor man of Europe. But it made it easier for me. Instead of feeling a poor traveller, I was a regular one.

So all I had to do was choose a place and a date. That year, I chose the South of France, Nice. I bought a return railway ticket for two weeks in July. One travel bag was enough. I didn't have many clothes in those days. I was getting ready for something. I am not sure what I was getting ready for. Nobody asked me, and I didn't ask myself. Luckily, nobody stopped me from going anywhere. At twenty-four, though still living at home, I had a job, I was considered adult. I was single, free, and a master of my fate.

When I got off the train at Nice, I called a taxi. I had not booked an hotel. In my precious school French, I asked the taxi-driver to stop by a hotel that was middle-sized, halfway between the town and the sea. He did, and soon I stepped out of the taxi with my small case. I was enfolded by the sweet warm air. I booked into the hotel in front of me. I will always remember the small room on the third floor, and my first look through the narrow window at the sea.

I spent the first few days exploring the town and the tidy beaches of Le Promenard des Anglais. I visited the church of the Sacred Heart at Audincourt to see the stained glass windows recently designed by Ferdinand Leger. I bought perfume in Vence. I visited Antibes. I enjoyed Mediterranean food in the cafes that local French people seemed to be using. I dozed on the beach in the afternoons, and acquired the essential sun-tan.

The book I had taken with me on holiday was written by Edgar Rice Burroughs. Most people know and have read his Tarzan books, but only an elete know about his Martian books. His hero, John Carter, has travelled to Arizona, to camp in the mountains under the shining light of the planet Mars. I knew from an earlier book that Carter had met a lovely princess on his first visit to Mars. She loved him, and was waiting for him to return to save her. Her name was Deja Thoris, and she was being kept prisoner somewhere among the dried-up river bottoms of Barsoom, one of the ancient oceans that were part of Mars before its centuries of drought. While he lay dreaming on his camp bed under the stars of Arizona, Carter felt irresistibly drawn to return to his chosen planet and waiting princess. By the end of the first chapter he had somehow been air-lifted through the vast sky above the mountains of Arizona to the surface of Mars, with very little boring physics in-between for me to deal with. Most of the book concerned the romantic task of finding and fighting for his loved one.

This story set my mood as I stood at the top of the hill looking down on Antibes. I was rested, sun-tanned, full of Mediterranean food and energy. I noticed a slight figure on a motor-bike climbing the long winding hill. The driver took the climb as fast as the bike would go, and with as much noise as the bike could make. At the top of the hill he drew in to the side, and stood up away from the machine. He was tall and slim, with a slight stoop. He wore gold-rimmed glasses under a mop of hair. He looked up to where I was standing, gave me a long look, caught my eye and smiled. After a moment he said a sentence in French into the silence. Would I like to join him on the back of the bike? John Carter thought nothing of travelling the millions of miles to Mars. What was this small journey compared to his, and to his battles to find his princess in Barsoom? I cannot remember if I answered in English or French, but in no time I was installed on the back seat of the motor-bike.

In those days we didn't have to bother about helmets. We circled carefully to the bottom of the hill, then it was the two of us against the forces of gravity and wind, climbing together, leaning in and out to the camber of the road as we climbed upwards as noisily as possible. At the top, I just nodded 'yes' as he indicated we should do the climb again, and again after that. Then we stepped off the bike, and in the pause and silence he suggested we went for a coffee. We found a small cafe he knew, parked the bike outside. French coffee and exotic pastries. I soon found that he was still at school, seventeen, and I was glad to tell him that I was twenty-four. We exchanged names. I cannot remember what his name was. When he suggested that we meet again next afternoon I was so happy. I was in love with him already.

We met next day outside the park he indicated. It was lovely to see him again, the slight figure, the mop of hair over the gold rims. We held hands as we walked, and mystic warmth enclosed us. As we were both using a language not our own, we didn't say much. Or perhaps we didn't need to say much. We were looking for a space in the world where we could be close. We explored every inch of the countryside. I was no longer looking for perfumes, church windows, tourist attractions. We were looking for green spaces away from the sight of others, where we could snuggle together. Perhaps because it was so difficult to find private space, the magnetism between us became stronger. After a while we more or less found a nook, and snuggled together, the half-dark surrounding us. I was used to snogging in the open, in woods and on beaches. It was my favoured habitat. I had read every book I could find by D.H. Lawrence. In his book 'Lady Chatterley', Mellors and Connie were happy enough on the grass in the woods. I accepted that world. In the countryside, sex could not be sweeter or more pure.

It was a revelation that I could be so drawn to a human being that I hardly knew. It was part of my world; perhaps it was not part of his. I was anxious to please, but it became clear that he was not able to make love in the woods in a way that suited his dreams.

By the end of the week he suggested that we book into a hotel for two hours. I have no idea how he could have acquired the knowledge at so early an age that such places existed, were possible. In spite of my doubts, that is what we did: we found ourselves in a very basic hotel for two hours. The situation seemed to please him, seemed to suit his needs. I will always have an aesthetic preference for nooks under the trees, but youth and passion carried us.

Meeting him every day defined that holiday. When the fortnight ended and I went home, we corresponded for a while in both languages.

As my tan faded, I was left with a sense of another milestone being passed. But it was hard to read what it said.

3

NO MORE KITTENS

THE DAY HAD come. She was sitting next to Luke, waiting for the London train that would take him to his university, where he would live in Halls. He was sitting at the far end of the seat, staring into space, already beginning his life away from her. An ideal relationship was ending. She had forgotten to breathe for moments; now the cool evening breeze carried the musty smell of city dust and engines. Her marriage to Luke's father had ended when Luke was six. The early years alone with a small child had been lonely ones. His childish chatter had often cut across her thoughts. The chatter had evolved into a meaningful exchange; the needy child had grown into an interesting companion. In the last years or so, Luke had begun to grow away from her. He had his own interests and friends.

The platform was becoming crowded. Other groups with bags and sports gear stood before them and the empty rails.

"Perhaps the kittens will be born by the time you get back to the house," said Luke.

"I think it will take longer than that."

Bessemer, their cat, had been promising kittens for days. She had obliged them many times before when they were needed, bringing warmth and gentleness in the desolate patches of their lives. Four kittens played in the basket when Luke was revising for O-levels, three during his A-levels. Other members of the family would call around and bask in the warmth of Bessemer's maternity. Talking about kittens became a bridge across difficult subjects over the years. But this time, when there was such a need, Bessemer had kept them waiting.

Now, Luke was pulling the train door shut. He stood framed by the window, a snapshot of himself. As they said their goodbyes she had an overpowering need to touch him, to stroke the warm corduroy. She raised her arm, then caught his expression and dropped it to adjust her scarf. Luke had learned the rules. It was not adult to show affection. When the train pulled away she stood for a while in the silence and emptiness left in its wake.

She had left a light on in the sitting-room, and raked up the coal fire in the hearth. For Bessemer's comfort, she had told herself.

"Hullo Bess. How have you been doing?" The cat looked up from her box alongside the fire, her stomach curving sumptuously. The box was lined with yesterday's

Guardian, and one of Luke's old sweaters. She cut up some cold chicken and placed it in the box, then went into the kitchen to wash up the dishes from their evening meal. She left one setting of plates and one knife and fork on the drainer; the rest she wiped and put away in the cupboard.

She went into Luke's room. The room looked bereft, like an old uniform stripped of its medals. Patches on the wall marked where the posters had been: empty spaces in the bookshelves gaped like missing teeth. She peeled the sheets off the bed, then made it up again with only the red woollen blankets. She smoothed her hand over the curve of marled wool.

Back in the living room, the cat seemed reassured by her presence and stretched out to its full length, turning its front paws up against the side of the box and splaying them out rhymically, sensuously, purring on a low rumbling note like thunder under water. She turned on the television: the news stitched a patchwork of strikes, sport and shootings. It seemed irrelevant.

After ten o'clock she phoned Luke to see if he had settled in. He was a long time answering. When he did, his voice sounded thin and distant. He seemed surprised that she had phoned.

She was conscious of the cat looking at her with narrowed eyes, needing her presence and attention. At regular intervals now a ripple of muscle would start in the shoulder region, and undulate down the furry body. The low purring continued. The sounds from the television distanced; more clearly she heard the rustle of newspapers under the cat's body, the cat's rumbled purr, the clock ticking, and her own breathing.

She envied the cat. It didn't need breathing exercises to relax. She remembered the exercises she had done when she was expecting Luke. "Breathe in deeply and relax every muscle as you slowly exhale." She had loved herself in those days; she had enjoyed and respected her body. "You must be tired carrying all that weight, mother," they had said at the clinic. But no, she had wanted to extend this happiest time of her life, when she had felt beautiful, useful and desirable, for as long as possible.

She put more coal on the fire and gazed, unfocussed, into the flames. She would have liked more children. But motherhood had already set up strains in their relationship. Her husband had seemed jealous of the little one, and had flirted with skinny friends when she was pregnant. She dared not risk her marriage again.

She bent down and smoothed the knobbly bone on top of the cat's head. It settled down further, using the sweater sleeve as a pillow, closing its eyes.

They both knew the sensuous pleasures of motherhood, the delights of breast-feeding where pain and pleasure fused into ecstasy.

She watched a wave of contractions move along the cat's body. The cat looked at her keenly. She bent down and took a front paw in her hand. The pads felt like loganberries surrounded by hooked thorns. She was pleased that the cat needed her, nourished by the rank smell of the fire-warmed fur.

Television had long lost its interest. One o'clock struck. Her knees were stiff. She felt she should stay with the cat until the kittens were born, but was tired. She got up quietly. The cat opened its eyes and looked anxious, but she deserted it for bed.

Her first thought was that she would be eating breakfast alone. Luke was in London, in another world. Then she thought about Bessemer.

The cat lay as she had left it. The kittens were born, but they were dead. Little tabby clones lay in a neat heap on the pink stained paper. Bessemer looked blank and detached, her teats swollen with milk.

She put the cat in the well-used cat-basket and drove to the vet. She left a name at the desk and took a seat, the basket on her knee. The woman next to her wore a hat. She carried a Siamese cat, wrapped in a shawl. The woman soon asked what was wrong with Bessemer.

"Oh. I couldn't stand all that messing in the house. I have my cats doctored. Females are expensive, but it's cheaper in the long run. Nicer. The males don't cost so much. It's just snipped off. Puts an end to all that noise, all that smell. I wouldn't put up with any of it."

"I quite like kittens," she said.

"There are too many strays running about as it is."

"I always find good homes for ours," she said.

Through the window in front of the basket she could see one of the cat's eyes, and one side of its mouth, with the speckled base for whiskers.

She got up quickly when her name was called. She carried the cat into the surgery, a practised owner. She undid the basket, lifted Bessemer onto the shiny table-top, and told the vet their troubles.

"How old is Cat?"

"Oh, seven or eight years"

"You know that's forty-nine for us humans. She's a middle-aged lady, and she's had enough families." He put his hand around the cat's haunches. "Her muscles are stretched and she can't give birth efficiently any more, can't nurture them. She's past it. Leave her now and we'll have her spayed. Come back in the afternoon; bring a blanket."

It was all she could do to concentrate on what he was saying. The vet put an arm on her shoulder He smiled a kind cheerful smile. "She won't feel anything. The stitches will be out in ten days. With no more kittens to wear her out, she'll be a new cat."

But she didn't want a new cat, she thought on the way out to the car. She said aloud, "I don't want a new cat. I liked the old one." She felt her own stomach muscles loosen and sag. The stretch marks that netted her stomach tingled. Her breasts felt heavy and burdensome. Spayed; poor dear. She would have to bury the dead kittens when she got home. There were no kittens and there never would be kittens. She would have to give the news to Luke when she phoned him. It was her personal failing. She and the cat were past it, spayed. The nest was empty, the biological clocks had stopped.

She drove past the pinched gardens. Adjusting the car mirror, she caught sight of her reflection. Her face looked strange and unfamiliar. Then the mirror slipped and her reflection slid away, leaving only a patch of morning sky with its small separate clouds. She felt weightless, an invisible female ghost.

It was over, the intensity of life of those fertile years. Over, the adventures, the sensuous pleasures of motherhood, the tenderness, the sense of renewal. Her child had grown up. There would be no more kittens.

4

GROWING UP

I<small>N THE SERIOUS</small> world of work and school, it seemed
so light-hearted, such fun, to make room for the two
squeaky little hamsters. A neighbour off on holiday was
glad enough to give them to us, together with their hutch,
complete with its tunnels and exercise wheel.

They soon became part of the household. Ben would
look forward to playing with them on his return from
infant school.

It was good for Ben, she thought. He would learn
some responsibility helping to feed his pets, and to clean
out their hutch.

The squeak of the wheel as it was turned by one little
animal or the other running around inside, and the seedy
smell, became part of the background of their lives. The
hamsters soon became tame, tame enough to be taken
out of their hutch.

That's how disaster struck. But it struck so quietly, so without warning. One minute Ben was holding one of the little creatures close to him, the next minute he tripped over the hutch, and fell heavily on top of it. The animal lay there silently. She waited for it to make a sound, to make a move. But it lay there silently.

Ben picked it up hopefully. It was limp.

"Wake it up, Mummy."

She took it from him. It was cool, cold, lifeless. "Oh dear, Ben, I'm afraid it's dead."

"He's asleep," he corrected her.

What could she say? He didn't know what 'dead' was.

"He won't wake up again."

"He will."

"This time, he never will." She felt the responsibility for explaining properly. It was an important happening. Death was a reality, a part of life, and this was Ben's first experience of it.

"As he is not going to wake up ever because he is dead, let us put him carefully in a box, and bury him somewhere nice where we can visit him."

"All right then." Ben looked glad to be doing something.

They found a shoebox, lined it with a last winter's vest, and put the limp furry body inside. They found a trowel, and carried the box to the nearby park. They spent some time finding what they both agreed was the right place for the burial. When all was done, they put some flowers on top of the earth.

For a while, the site was a place to visit when they went to the park.

The surviving hamster must have felt lonely on his own. But he went on exercising on the wheel, exploring the tunnels, hiding food in his cheeks as hamsters do. It was a good year later before he died, this time from natural causes, although they didn't know what these were.

"Here we go again," she said to Ben, when they took the limp body out of the hutch, and laid it on the kitchen floor, "Shall we take him down to the park and bury him?"

Ben looked at the small body coolly. "No need to bother," he said, "He's dead."

"What shall we do with him then?

"We could just put him in the bin."

She felt a mixture of relief, and something else.

She looked at Ben. If he could accept the fact of death, she would have to accept that he was growing up,

5

THE FACTS OF LIFE

WHERE DID BABIES come from? I didn't know, and my sister didn't know. But we had a stroke of good luck in the family. I overheard someone say that my father's sister was pregnoss. I passed this information on to my sister. "Preg what, stupid?" said my sister. "Well, then I heard them say that because she's getting on past forty, it's probably the menopass."

"Oh well that's it then."

But she got through it and went on to have the baby, at home. That Sunday, we were all to visit. We were going to the very source of knowledge, and we made up our minds to take this chance and ask where babies came from.

"You girls are to have your hair washed, and behave yourselves if you want to come with us and be introduced to your little cousin."

So we stood, well behaved and hair shining, at the side of the bed, with the impossibly small baby sleeping in its cot. I looked at my sister, and she looked back at me. I usually did the talking. "Auntie, where do babies come from?" My aunt sighed. She looked over at my mother. We all seemed to be looking at each other in that silent room. At last my aunt said, "From under the gooseberry bush in the garden. I thought all little girls knew that." Soon they were discussing possible names, and that was that.

As we walked back home, my sister said, "I know they come from the chemist. I heard Uncle say that he was given a prescription to take to the chemist, and he had to wait for it to be made up." A chemist seemed a more likely place. It was clean and dry. Better there than to be left out in the garden in all weathers.

My education continued a few years later. In those days before the war, it was usual to employ young girls from distant valley towns to 'live in' and do most of the housework. My mother considered it bountiful to employ a young person who applied for the job, and who, we gathered, had a 'past.' We didn't know what the 'past' was, but overheard some of her friends warn, "It isn't wise to have that sort of person mixing with the girls. Remember the nits last term."

But we took to Gertie. She told us lively stories about people and places in a broad Welsh accent. There were dire warnings.

"Men? They're no good. No good. And don't you believe a word they say to you. Not one word I tell you."

"What did they say to you Gertie?"

"My Gwillym it was. He told me I was beautiful."

"Well you are."

"Oh yes. And he said, you are the only girl in the world for me. I will love you forever. All my life I will just love you."

"For ever? And did he?"

"No he did not. He took me out. Many's the time we went out together when we were courting."

"Where did he take you? To parties and theatres and to the pictures?"

"Not often. No-o. Into the woods mostly, and in the back of the car when it was cold. There were presents on my birthday. I thought to myself, I thought, I have found the love of my life. I'm going to be married. I dreamed of the lovely white dress I would wear on the day."

"We've got lots of drawings of our wedding dresses too. I'll bring them to show you."

"I don't want to see them. It's not lucky."

"Then what happened. What happened then?"

"Then I told 'im I were pregnant. I never saw 'im again."

"Never saw him?"

"Never."

On winter days, Gertie would talk to us. I remember one wet Monday after school. I sat on the third stair as I often did. My sister was half way up in the shadows behind me. Gertie was kneeling in the hall on a thin sponge by her bucket of hot water. " Baby hospital is a scary place." She had a scrubbing brush in her right hand. She rubbed this onto a block of Sunlight soap, then began to soap over a patch of red and blue quarry tiles. She was a master of this craft. As well as following her words, I was mesmerised by her skill. She selected a section of tiles, and began covering them with soapy water. She scrubbed vigorously with the long end of the brush to form a firm froth of soapy suds. Then she dipped her floor-cloth in the clear hot water, wrung it out with all the strength of both hands until it was drained pale, and mopped up the scrubbed suds to disclose an area of clean tiles underneath. "Women are left in those beds in terrible pain hour after hour." She selected the next patch of dirty floor. "The mothers lie in those beds without love or care. Babies are born without doctors there."

"Where are the doctors?"

"They don't bother to come out for single mums. They run out of gas and air but no-one bothers. We were there in the dark for hour after hour."

"Didn't he ever come. The one who loved you?"

"No, 'e never come."

"You were alone."

"No-o. I were not alone. There were other women next to me along the ward at different stages. If a woman cried out too loud, a nurse would wheel the bed into another room. Never saw them again. And somewhere there was holy mother Mary, mother of God. We all cried out to her."

"I'm glad she was there."

Gertie put her brush down for a moment, and straightened her back. She looked at me to read my expression. When she sat up, the late sun shone through the glass front door to form a halo of white light around her head. The sweat on her forehead and cheeks glowed like varnish. She looked like an angel in a painting.

My mother thought it a mitzvah to have Gertie to 'live in.' It was. When my sister and I dated our boy-friends in those days before the pill, my mother worried with the best of her friends about us getting pregnant. But while the red and blue quarry tiles in our hall gleamed with scrubbing, the chance of that happening was absolutely nil.

6

ONE SATURDAY AFTERNOON

THE LONG WEEK of school seemed endless, but thank goodness, Saturday arrived at last. I walked over to the shop at the top of the street to do important shopping, a precious two shillings and sixpence heavy in my pocket. I smelt again that familiar earthy smell of old potatoes. There, on the middle shelf, I could see copies of the Hotspur, The Wizard, the Beano, the Dandy, one pile layered over the other waiting for me to choose. I had tried them all. Some were good for school stories, some were good for adventure, but it was the Beano I fancied today. I picked up a copy lovingly, and took it to the counter.

"Wouldn't you rather read one of these, luv?" said the shop-keeper. His bony wrist emerged from a biscuit coloured overall, "More your kind of thing I would have thought." He pointed to the next shelf of girl's comics, with their pretty covers and tempting offers of hair slides and lipsticks.

"Oh no, I can't be bothered with that lot, they're for cissies." My eyes scanned the counter for bars of chocolate. There they were, in perfect lines, in immaculate dark purple wrappers. "And a bar of Cadbury's please."

I went out into the eternal sunshine making for home, past the parked bicycles falling over the pavement, the junk shop, the grocery shop, the empty boarded-up shop with a Chad drawn across the door. I crossed the road, stepping over the hopscotch chalk marks on the pavement, back to the cool dark of my house. I slid my hand through the letter-box to pull the string that opened the front door.

There was no one in the front room. The room was fairly tidy. It was only used for visitors, and for piano practice. But now it was empty. I sank onto the settee to inspect my goodies. The best moment of the week had arrived. I opened the comic and flicked through it. I had been following a serial story in this paper. There it was, 'The Ant World,' where two scientists had become small by accident last week, and so were able to explore inside an ant heap, meeting terrible dangers. They had been captured by ants, put into cages, and used as pets for the young ants. The paper was warm and smooth under my fingers. I breathed in printing ink mixed with the tar from cigarette stubs left in the ash-tray.

I leaned against the back of the old settee in the quiet room. My father was at work. There were small movements from the kitchen in the back of the house where my mother was working quietly. I didn't know where my brothers and sister had gone. Nobody bothered about where I was or what I was doing. Outside I could hear distant rumblings from lorries on their interminable journeys along the new motorway. The separate sounds were mixed into a hum, muffled as if through water. I was safe and alone and free. Nothing was expected of me for this day.

I dipped into my pocket and drew out the bar of chocolate. On the purple cover, two glasses of milk were being poured. I slipped the paper jacket off the silver with care, and tore a small section of the foil that clung to a chocolate square at the top. It gave softly under my thumb to reveal an impression of the little letters incised on the dark chocolate beneath:

'Cadburys,' it read. As I peeled off this last barrier, the ineffable smell of chocolate lifted into the air in warm waves.

I flattened the page on my lap. The Ant World lay before me with all its wonder and mystery. I was about to enter the ant heap. There was no sound from the house, only the low grumbles from the distant traffic. I breathed in deeply and, putting the first smooth square of chocolate into my mouth, began to read.

7

BEHIND THE SMILE

THE DENTIST CAME from behind me, holding a syringe. "The injections will be a bit painful, but from then on you will feel nothing." And there it was, a series of sharp needle flashes that filled my universe for a few moments.

"Very good," said the dentist. "Now sit quietly in the waiting room for ten minutes. It's a slow acting injection, but very efficient."

I sat on the deep cushioned sofa in the waiting room and waited. I had already waited some years for today. I flicked over the magazines on the low table in front of me. They were classy ones, the clothes magazines showed expensive clothes, and the housekeeping ones, expensive homes. This was an expensive dentist. But the magazines didn't take my interest. Instead, I leaned back into the deep cushions and sank into reverie.

I remembered my first meeting with Sinjeon at our local swimming pool. He was there by the pool with my best friend, Sonia, when I arrived. I waved over to her, finished the lengths I had set myself, and climbed out of the water to join them on the pool-side, cool and dripping. Sonia introduced us.

"Meet Sinjeon. He's social secretary at Uni. this year."

Sinjeon had a friendly smile, and a gentle low voice. No wonder he was social secretary. I'd vote for him.

Then later over hot drinks, Sonia suggested we got a party together at her house for her seventeenth birthday.

On the day of the party, I went shopping for a new dress. I took ages trying to find one I liked, gave up, and in end, wore an old one. I arrived at the party feeling drab and flustered.

Sonia opened the door. "You could have made an effort to come early and give me a hand." So I felt guilty as well.

The party merged into friendly chaos. Sonia suggested party games, and switched the music on.

"Get into circles, girls in the middle, boys outside." We started moving clockwise.

"When the music stops, kiss the person opposite you."

The music stopped. Sinjeon was opposite me. He smiled his friendly smile, approached me slowly, hands on my shoulders. "Hullo you," he said. I looked into his eyes. I can see them now, blue-green with an outside ring of black. My first kiss. The warm silk of his lips on the silk of mine, then I was drawn closer. My being dissolved into an abyss. Behind my closed eyes, stars sparkled and flashed. The music sighed, then moved on and parted us. The rest of the evening was a haze. Sinjeon was a hit with me, but I didn't know what his side of the kiss was like. A girl called Julie with long fair hair who told funny jokes seemed to amuse him. I found parties confusing, and was glad when it was time to go. We filed into Sonia's bedroom to collect our coats.

Sonia had a photograph of me on her mantle-piece along-side pictures of her pets and holiday snaps. This one of me was smiling, showing lots of teeth. In those days, my teeth were as white as I could make them, but the front ones were uneven. Julie picked up this photo and said, "Have you Macleaned your teeth today?" - a bye-line of the time. Sinjeon came to look, and the photo was passed around a giggling group.

The teasing phrase and the laughter were small sharp knives that pierced my body.

The next day, my mother remarked how quiet I was. I was past confiding in her. She seemed to think parties were fun and games. She didn't know they were issues of life and death. I was brooding on my plainness. I couldn't hope to attract Sinjeon, or any boy-friend, with my looks as they were. And especially my teeth. But I could do something about those. It was too late to have them straightened, but I would do whatever the film-stars did when I could afford it. I saw a glossy advertisement that promised to improve your smile, with before and after photographs, and that was it. I inquired how much it would cost, and I was given film-star prices. But I was going to do it whatever the cost. I would work and save, and by the time Julie's teeth went black and fell out, I would have improved my smile. I was still dreaming when the dentist called me in.

As I settled into the chair, the dentist warned me. "Now you won't feel this now, as your mouth is numb, but it will be quite painful afterwards for a day or so."

My mouth was open so I couldn't answer him. I could have told him it would be as nothing to the pain I felt on the day of that party.

8

THE BRAMBLE BUSH

IT WAS ONLY weeks to Christmas. Ceri sat at her desk in the third form class-room, waiting for something exciting to happen. Mrs Morse was standing in front with a book in her hand, about to start the lesson. She had opened her mouth to begin - what was she going to say? - when there was a tip-tap on the door; in came Miss James and that was the end of that. The two teachers had a lot to say with their heads close together. Miss James was taking a sheaf of typed papers out of her case. They both went to the high desk and laid out the papers.

"We are selecting people for the Sleeping Beauty panto," said Miss James. She read from a list of names of the pupils in her class. She called out the names and the parts they were to play for almost everyone. At last, Ceri heard her own name called. "And Ceri will be the lilac fairy."

She couldn't believe it. She loved the colour lilac, and to be the fairy! With luck there wouldn't be too many words to learn, just a dance in a lovely lilac dress. She couldn't wait till the end of the class, the end of the day, and the sound of the bell. Soon she was bouncing on air, almost flying home with the wonderful news.

"I'm to be the lilac fairy in the panto this year." She twirled on her toes.

Her mother said, "That's fine. I'll get a few yards of gauzy material for your costume and you'll look even more like a fairy princess than you do already." And soon the sitting room was awash with lovely lilac-coloured material, and she was being measured and draped with the soft magic of dreams.

She went to bed as light as a fairy, but she woke up next morning feeling a heavy earth-being. Then when she looked at herself in the mirror to see who she was, she saw the big red spots on her face and on her chest and more or less everywhere.

Her mother said, "Oh my, you've got chicken pox, like your friend Mary down the road. Just as well to have it over with. No school for a few days until the spots all go away and you are back to yourself again."

It wasn't too long before she was well, and back at her desk in school. The lilac costume was all finished, and she really wanted to live in it, it was so soft and filmy. It was all she could do to wear her uniform to school today. She was a fairy, she didn't feel a schoolgirl any more.

Mrs Morse said, "I'm glad you're better Ceri. Now you know that the show must go on, and as you were ill, Jennifer kindly agreed to take the part of the lilac fairy."

"But it's all right Mrs Morse, I'm better now, and the dress is finished and everything."

"Thank you for being such a brave little trouper, but we need you to be a green gardener, to tend the bramble bushes, along with Mario, Elizabeth, Brian, Jenny and David. They will show you what to do."

All the lights seemed to go out, all the lights in the world. Every joy she had ever had, every birthday candle waiting to be blown, every hug of love, all shrivelled now into a burning, aching fire in the very centre of her body, and she knew her life would never be happy again, never, never. Yet she couldn't cry or tell of the pain, because that wasn't what you did. You were to be a brave trouper, so you just felt it inside and stayed still and silent.

Mrs Morse went on talking. She heard the voice from her private zone of pain, coming from a vast distance. "Now I want all you actors to remember that we are building up a magic world for our audience. I know that your parents will be there looking out for you, but whatever you do, no-one must turn around out of character to wave to their family. Now Jennifer, could you tell us what it is we must not do."

The horrible Jennifer repeated, "We must not turn around and wave from the stage to people we know."

Her mother did her best to cheer her up, to make a green dress that fitted, but Ceri did not enjoy wearing the new dress at all, and could not be cheered. She hated green and always would. Besides, it was made of ordinary gardeners' material and five others were wearing the same style, so where was the magic in that? All the magic seemed to have gone from her life, and when could it ever come back?

The dress rehearsal was an especially sad day. It was bleak and windy outside, and inside, the stage was heavy with a circle of foliage in many shades of green that she and the other gardeners were to tend and cultivate.

Mrs James reminded them, "Now remember, actors. This is a magic wood. Do not look at your parents or wave to them whatever you do." And suddenly, Ceri could see a pale ray of light shining through the brambles.

At last performance day came. Sleeping Beauty was there on the stage, the wicked grandmother, the hated Jennifer. Somewhere was the prince, outside the draped green bramble bushes they were tending, seeking his princess. Ceri could hear the mean words again, "Do not turn and wave to your parents." The last few words echoed around the stage, around her head, "Turn and wave to your parents." Well, why not, they had worked hard enough for this performance: her father had left his business early, her mother had made not one, but two costumes. "Wave to your parents."

So Ceri rustled the drapes of green bush and turned and waved to her parents, who she could just see through the foot-lights, and they waved back. And one by one the other gardeners turned around in the drapes of green and waved to their parents, until the gardeners were all waving together from the shaking bramble bushes so it no longer looked like a bush and all the magic must certainly have left the wood. Especially when her parents, followed by the rest of the audience, started laughing and clapping, and they all stood up and cheered.

The magic was not all lost. Somehow it was flowing back again, onto the stage and into the world.

9

THE NEW TERM

THE COPPER-COLOURED ALARM clock with the big bells could be relied on to wake him early. When the two bells exploded into ringing, he was already awake. This day marked a new beginning, and being on time was top of the list of changes to be made.

His school shirt was on its hanger at the foot of his bed. It was clean, but not ironed. The creases would come out while he wore it.

He was washed and dressed in minutes. It took even less time to grab a slice of bread and spread it with margarine. He longed to have a cooked breakfast, and even more than that, to share the company of his mother.

But during his time at secondary school, that hadn't happened. His mother wasn't well, in a way he didn't understand. She was up and about when he came home, but anxious and depressed. He missed her in the mornings.

He left the grey sadness of his home behind him as he went out into the morning street.

The walk to school was about a mile, and he had ways to while away the journey. Sometimes he walked only on pavement squares, sometimes only on lines. Today, he had found a small stone and kicked it along the wet gutter. Well, he was in good time today. This was the first day of a new term, and the first day of his new life plan. He was going to do things differently this year. He was going to work harder and learn stuff. He was going to change from 'slow learner, could do better. to 'hard worker, much improved'. He had reached the school entrance now; he flipped the stone into the next drain grating. He would never see it again.

He entered through the side gate, into the familiar smell of Jeyes fluid and chalk. He crossed the polished wood-block floor to his new class-room.

Things would be different this year. He used to sit at the back, talk to his friends, and read his Beano. Not any more. Now he chose a central desk right at the front of the room. The others arrived in ones and twos. The classroom gradually filled up. The form tutor arrived and took his place in the facing desk, in front of the blackboard. David was sorry to note that it was Mr Menzies from last year. At 8.30 exactly, as they heard the chimes from the city hall clock, he said, "Good Morning Class 11."

"Good morning, Mr Menzies."

Mr Menzies opened the register and started to call the names.

David felt a familiar ache of anxiety. He stuttered sometimes, and when his name was called he would need to answer promptly. He breathed in deeply now, and rehearsed his answer silently.

At last his name, and he heard himself answer, "P.p.p..." Mr Menzies gave him a long suffering look, his pen poised.

"P.p.p... resent." He breathed out in relief as other names were called. He told himself he didn't care. Things would be different this year. He would take careful notes, do his homework at the proper time, read around the subject. It must feel great to be top of the class. He began to imagine it: sitting an exam, being able to answer every question. Then, the results coming in. He had been awarded top marks. He was carrying the results home in an envelope. He was telling his father. He was watching his father's face change from surprise to joy. He saw the pride on his mother's face. He was lost in a day-dream of hope and promise.

He heard the form master say, "Now, if David Capel would be good enough to take that simpering smile off his face, we will make a start." The class tittered. Then, David knew it was not going to happen. He would not be able to concentrate on lessons. He didn't manage to grasp much of what he was told in class last year, and it would be no better this year. No wonder this tutor despised him. At the end of each day he would take home notes of lessons he had not understood, and no-one would be able to help him do his homework. No one would care.

The day stretched ahead, with only the long walk back to a grey home and a sad mother at the end of it. After that was the endless term, and somewhere in a haze was the end of the year. His future years disappeared into the darkness of a collapsed tunnel.

10

DYLAN AND ME

PEOPLE WHO KNOW me well, know I had a meeting in my past with the poet, Dylan Thomas.

It all happened when I was younger and even lovelier than I am today. We met up, Dylan and me. This is how it happened.

I got off the train at Paddington and called a taxi.

"Mandrake club please, it's in Soho."

"I know where it is, miss."

It was good to be back in London again. I was looking forward to meeting a friend and visiting exhibitions. I savoured the familiar landmarks. We drew up at a shabby building. It was eight o'clock, just getting dark. I swung around the railings and down the littered stone stairway to the basement. It was a club of easy membership, used by writers and artists. The L-shaped bar-room was dimly lit except for a scattering of red glowing lamps, veiled by stale smoke. I sat on a bar stool and ordered a pint of bitter. Beer was cheap in the fifties. I was early; I had an hour to wait for my friend. I looked for a seat at one of the tables. By the wall was a longish table with only three people sitting at it. I carried my glass to the unoccupied end.

I am afraid of many things: spiders, lifts, magnifying mirrors. But I am not afraid to travel alone. I can sit alone in a crowd happily, and dream.

A voice from the end of the table said, "Alone tonight, cariad?"

I looked up. It was Dylan Thomas. I recognised him from the portrait by Alfred Janes that hangs in our museum in Cardiff. But since that portrait was painted, the curves on his cheeks and chin had deepened and the mouth had loosened. I took a long drink.

His voice from the shadows was warm gravy brown, "Come back to my rooms tonight and sleep with me?"

"Thank you very much for the invitation, but no."

"You are the only healthy-looking person in this room. You are the only one I fancy."

"That's because I've just arrived from Cardiff where the air is fresher."

"Oh, from Wales is it then?" He took a long draught from his handled glass. "So how about a cwtch with me tonight - human on my faithless arm?" The liquid gleamed wetly from his lower lip.

"Thank you, but no cwtches."

"You've only got this one chance. I'm leaving for Persia tomorrow for a poetry reading."

"Are you flying by magic carpet?"

His lower lip fluttered. "I am travelling by BOAC." He waved his glass, "Look, if you stay tonight, you will be able to tell your friends that you slept with Dylan Thomas."

"And if I don't stay, I'll be able to tell my friends that Dylan Thomas asked me to sleep with him, and I refused."

I thought I had been so clever all these years, till I heard from dear Germaine Greer.

She went to a party and met Enricho Fellini, who fancied her. He turned up at her flat with a slim suitcase carrying - his brown silk pyjamas. What Germaine Greer has known for half her life, I will never know.

I will never know the colour of Dylan Thomas's pyjamas.

11

MY BEST HOLIDAY
IN THE WORLD

DID YOU HAVE a good holiday this year? Well, don't tell me about it. I don't want to know. This is a bad time of the year for me. People are coming back from their holidays. I am glad to see them back, but they are all lining up to tell me how marvellous their holidays were. It's getting worse. Friends used to tell me about their trips to Spain, to France, to Italy. Now they are travelling further. People are coming back from the Galapagos islands with tales of turtles, the Poles with tales of penguins, and beyond. There is the inevitable listing of aeroplane journeys, of muddy carbon footsteps around the world, and of money spent. My cousin Rita said she had run out of world.

I've had enough. It's my turn to tell you about *my* best holiday. No carbon footprints: the only steps were in our local sand. I went to Llangeneth, one of those heavenly beaches along the Gower coast, in Wales, and I got there by bus.

We were twenty-something, my sister Zara and I. She was having her first holiday away from home with cousin Maurice, whom she later married. I was supposed to be some sort of chaperone. When the three of us arrived, we asked in the local shop in the square opposite the King's Head pub, about somewhere to stay. They gave us the address of a bed and breakfast in the village. That is where the magic began.

I can't remember the name of the street we stayed in, and I expect it's long changed, so this won't send a lot of adventurers to find it. We ended in a dear little stone cottage with small rooms and no electricity. We came back from a day of exploring the beaches to a neat front room with a green -baize covered table. In the centre of the table was a paraffin lamp. Here we had our evening meal. Each day we were asked what we wanted cooked, we paid for the shopping, and a hot meal was put on the table as we sat around it in the evening. No electricity, but in the morning, a china bowl and hot water in a flowery jug were brought up to us in our rooms, the flower-sprigged curtains drawn back.

And the day was ours. I don't know if you are familiar with the beaches along that coast. Next to Llangeneth is Oxwich, and my favourite, Three-cliffs Bay with its freshwater stream and crumbling castle. I got to know every mossy pool, every sand-dune, and every cave. There were huge, harmless, flat jelly-fish left high and dry on the water's edge among the shoals of seaweed, and amazing shells. After high tides our feet scrunched through flotsam and jetsam left along the shoreline. There were fishermen's nets, green balls, and sea-treasure for no one but us to discover. It was an isolated place in those days before cars, before the dunes were opened into a caravan park and camp-site. We could have been on a desert island miles from civilization in the silence and isolation.

By the end of a day of beach wandering, when I usually went my own way, I sensed the peace, the peace of paradise. We returned to our stone cottage for a hot meal in the dark curtained front room, to sit in the glow of the paraffin lamp.

Are you the same as I am about reading? Every holiday I can remember is linked to the book I took with me at the time.

The book I took with me on this best holiday in the world was Captain Scott's Journals: the 'Worst Journey in the world'. His writing and the beaches will be linked in my memory forever. I began reading in the glow of that precious paraffin lamp. As I sat at the table at the end of the day inhaling the warm friendly smell of burning oil, I absorbed the words from Scott's diary. He had set sail for the Antarctic in his ship, 'Terra Nova'. They called at Cardiff Dock to load up with coal. I had first learned about him from the plaque on the lighthouse in our Roath Park Lake. It described them as very gallant gentlemen'. He was already my hero. His diary was found with him, under his frozen body in the tent where he and the last three explorers died on the trek home.

I first related to him through his attitude to dogs. Nansen had advised him to take dogs on the journey, to use them for pulling supplies, then to eat them afterwards. How I saw it, Scott was too English to do this, it didn't appeal to him, and so he died. I loved him for that.

His first entry was dated: *"Saturday, December 1912: Stayed on deck till midnight. The sun just dipped below the southern horizon. The scene was incomparable. The northern sky was gloriously rosy. And reflected in the calm sea between the ice, which varied from burnished copper to salmon pink: bergs and pack to the north had a pale greenish hue with deep purple shadows, the sky shaded to saffron and pale green. We gazed long at these effects. Morning found us pretty well at the end of the open water.'*

I enjoyed another long day on the beach. Then that evening around the paraffin lamp, after our meal, I read on: -

'A ship going through the pack must either break through the floes, push them aside, or go around them. When the floes are pressed together it is difficult and sometimes impossible to force a way through, but when there is a release of pressure the sum of many little gaps Just when I thought it safe to go up to bed, they pass two more immense bergs: 'It seemed impossible that the ship could win her way through them.' At last the team was able to get clear of bergs and

land themselves, their gear, and their dog sleds on to the icy shore of Ross Island.

By the end of the next day I was able to read, 'The light was good at first, but rapidly grew worse till we could see nothing of the surface of the ice. The dogs showed signs of wearying. We were running by the sledges. Suddenly Wilson shouted "Hold on to the sledge," and I saw him slip a leg into a crevasse. Five minutes later, as the teams were trotting from side to side, the middle dogs of our team disappeared. In a moment, the whole team was sinking - two by two - we lost sight of them, great strength and kept a foothold. The sledge stopped and we leaped aside. We had actually been travelling along the ridge on a crevasse, the sledge had stopped on it, and the dogs hung in their harness in the abyss, suspended between the sledge and the leading dog. Why the sledge and ourselves didn't follow the dogs we shall never know. We hauled the sledge clear of the bridge and anchored it. The dogs were howling dismally. It took hours to rescue them, secure them to the main trace, set up camp and get a hot meal.'

Next morning I was so glad to be back on the warm sand with no cares of dogs or provisions. The sea was cool and salty. The sand shelved very gradually, and I lay dreaming, half in the cool water, half warmed by the sun in the shallow waves, without a care in the world throughout the long day. I spent hours looking into rock pools in the warm sunshine.

It was not until I got back to the cottage and to my book at the end of the day that I realised that things were really going downhill for my heroes.

On page 404, 'The Last March', they are returning from the Pole. They had been hit by the awful realisation that Amundsen had got to the Pole first, and had planted the Norwegian flag and a letter to their king to prove it. It was downhill from then on.

'Misfortunes rarely come singly. At the Middle Barrier depot we found a shortage of oil. With rigid economy it can scarcely take us to the next depot on this surface. Second, Oates disclosed his feet, the toes, frost-bitten by the late temperatures, looking very bad indeed. The third blow showed in the night, the wind which we had hailed with joy, brought dark overcast weather. "It fell below -40 degrees in the night, and this morning it took one and a half hours to get our foot gear on."

Worse was to come — "The surface is simply awful. In spite of strong winds and full sail, we have only done five miles. The surface is covered with a thin layer of woolly crystals that cause impossible friction to the runners. On the surface we are cheerful, but what each man feels in his heart I can only guess. We are about 42 miles from the next depot, but with only 3-4 days fuel. Shall we get there?"

At the depot at last, there was cold comfort, there had been a leaking of oil from the cans." Poor Oates is unable to pull, barely able to walk. Nothing could be said but to urge him to march as long as he could. But when he awoke in the morning it was blowing a blizzard. He said, 'I am just going outside and may be some time.' He went out into the blizzard, and we have not seen him since."

The weather doesn't give us a chance. Got within 11 miles of the next depot but had to lay up all night because of a severe blizzard. No fuel and only one or two days of food left - must be near the end.

Then, *Thursday March 29th, we have had a continuous gale. We had fuel to make two cups of tea and barely food for two days, but we cannot move from our tent. Outside the tent we are stopped by a scene of whirling drift. It is a pity, but I do not think I can write more. For God's sake, look after our people."*

It was a tragedy of course. But there is something in the nature of tragedy that is uplifting. I felt blessed by the bravery they had shown, and by the life you have. I felt warmed by the sun, calmed by the holiday, in love with my lost heroes.

Now, at the end of the week, I was ready to leave my lovely beaches, gather my books, and go home.

12

A WALK OVER
THE BEACONS

IT WAS THE end of the first year at Art School. Exams were over and there was spring in the air. I had little money for travel, but lots of energy, so I planned a hostelling holiday with two fellow students, Gwenda and June.

I had been invited to Gwenda's house at half-term, and explored the coal-blackened, narrow streets of Abertillery, where she lived with her grand-parents. Knowing her was like finding an exquisite jewel long protected by a Welsh Baptist cradling. "I'm not expected home," she had said on the last day of term. "I'll walk anywhere." June endured the sedate boredom of her parents' home in a neat, cream-painted semi in Canton, Cardiff. "I could do with a sketching trip." She was a promising student; she travelled with her sketchbook and basic drawing materials at the ready.

None of us were serious walkers, so we planned a modest ten miles or so over the Brecon Beacons. We arrived at base by bus. I carried an Ordnance map. We straggled over the steep side of the mountain, making for a stream that led to a track that led to a wood that should lead to Storey Arms, the youth hostel where we planned to stay. We found the stream. The morning air blowing from the rippling water was intoxicating with its sweetness and promise after the petrol fumes and dust of the city. Behind me, the others looked like wild flowers spread out along the banks, with their bright hand-knits, patched jeans and makeshift rucksacks.

We soon got lost; one track looked so much like another, but we carried on climbing higher, over one hill after another. Each time we climbed to the top of a hill we looked over to see another slightly higher one ahead of us.

We stopped to rest on the wiry, cropped grass, and got out our apples and bottles of juice. I spread out the map again, and stared at it for clues about our position.

June said, "I don't think you are all that good at map-reading. I was quite impressed at first."

I gave up trying to identify our position on the map, and folded it up along its seams. "It will be useful for sitting on."

I remember the sun on my face and shoulders, after the long days indoors. It was meltingly, intensely warm. On the slope of the hill, walking at an angle to the earth,

I felt so much closer to the sun. Our feet grew worn and tired, and we shared our grumbles. June was too busy pausing to sketch to notice her feet. She stood poised over her sketch-book with a heavy curtain of hair draped over one eye, pointing out that it was the way that the hills were layered one behind the other, their colour cooled to a blue haze, that gave a sense of distance.

More than once, at the top of yet another look-alike hill, we were drenched by a welcome mist that became rain. Then the sun would dry us. We seemed to have been walking forever. When we looked back, the hills behind us looked so like the hills in front. At last we found the five-bar gate that was marked on the map. As we climbed the gate one by one I noticed how long our shadows had become. We had been walking all day. None of us had walked so far in our lives. Then a faint track appeared in the wilderness ahead of us. It became more marked and opened onto a stony road. We were near civilisation at last. A welcome sign-post said 'Ystradfellte', and underneath, a piece of weathered wood in the shape of a hand pointed to the Y.H.A. We were glad to check into that hostel in the small village. It was the next hostel to Storey Arms. We realised that we had walked much further than planned.

We seemed to be the only visitors. Simple food was offered: bacon, eggs and toast, and it tasted wonderful. Wales could be relied on for all day breakfasts if nothing else. Then we sat in the bare women's dormitory, with our feet in basins of cold water. Men were allocated a separate dormitory in those days.

Later that evening we heard male voices from the men's side, through the thin partition. I could make out different voices - four or five perhaps. Somehow a conversation started up between us. It started up in a giggly, teasing way.

"How do we know you're real people in there?" we said, "You could be mountain ghosts."

"Mountain goats? We'll go along with that."

"You could be the green men we've heard about. It's just the sort of place green men would come from."

"We're more suntanned than green at the moment. I don't think green men ride bikes"

"Di's looking a bit green. But he had a few too many ciders at the last pub."

Gradually, the voices through the wall thinned out, and one by one my friends went off to bed. But one voice on the other side remained. It was warm and had a Welsh lilt. We slowly got to know each other, me and the voice. In the quiet half-dark we exchanged ideas and dreams. I drew my basin of cold water nearer to the partition, my feet swished in the water, and my head rested on the thin partition while we talked in low voices. I found I was confiding more of myself than I usually did. We talked long into the night, relaxed disembodied spirits. We might have been the only beings left in the world.

"Have you been climbing other places?" he asked

"No, I'm not that much into climbing."

"Well, you've heard of the man who spent a whole night alone at the top of Cader Idris, by the side of the lake."

"That's a magic thought. Not the climbing, but the experience of being in a place like that on your own."

"They say if you spend the night there on your own, by the morning you'll be either a poet or mad."

"You'd certainly be changed."

"Perhaps I would become mad. I'm a poet already."

"Published?"

"Small presses. What would we do without them? But I'm waiting for a collection of my poems to come out soon."

" What are your poems about?"

"The usual themes. Love, loneliness, awareness of space and time. Mountains. It's so much better to sit at the top of a mountain waiting for inspiration than to sit in your room at home."

"Where no wind blows."

"That's quite a poetic line. Are you a poet?"

"No. A painter perhaps. That's what I'm studying to do." We were quiet for a while. Then I said, "We are lucky to live here in Wales. The mountains are soaked in poetry and beauty. And rain. Not that I've travelled far, but I can't imagine a lovelier place. I would like to find that sunken village marked on my map, where families lived and worked until it was submerged to make a reservoir for towns-people."

"That's not so far from here."

"I would look deep into the waters, and imagine the sunken town transformed by time, water, and fable into an eternal city under the lake."

"Where people still live?"

"Of course."

"The lost City of Atlanta, in Wales."

"Just a minute." The water in the bowl was feeling cold. I shook my feet free of the water and found a towel in my rucksack to fold them into. My feet were glowing. The strip of wood I had been leaning on was hard, and smelt of preservative. I shifted to rest on the other cheek. There were small sounds from the others, but they were the sounds that sleepers make, sighs and deep breathing. "I'm still here. Are you still there?"

"I've been writing a poem."

I heard the sound of scribbling behind the wooden partition.

"Why don't we go together and sit beside the lake at the top of the mountain?"

"In the morning we would be mad, or poets."

"We would be in love." She heard more scribbling behind the wood.

"Hold the presses." My poem starts, 'I want to walk with you my love over the Black Mountains, to watch the sunrise.' "Get ready for the next line…" Then there were more sounds of writing, and of paper being crumpled.

"Are you still there?"

"I'm still here. Here is the last verse. 'Come with me and set our tent on the Black Mountains. We will live on wild fruits, the juice of lemons raw, and milk, and bathe in pools of rain. Live on rough grass close to the moon, where the earth is sere and bare. There be my love, and be my love again.' It needs some rewriting."

"Not too much. It's a dream of a poem. But perhaps better not to go tonight. It's almost dawn. Better sleep while we can."

I barely recognised my reflection next morning. Exposure to the sun and rain had wrought a sea-change. My hair was usually curled to make a tidy shape around my head. Now it was bleached pale by the sun and sprang away from my forehead. My eyes shone strangely blue through the sunburnt skin. I couldn't bear bra-straps on my shoulders, my free breasts were outlined under my tee-shirt.

I felt good as I went down to breakfast with the others.

I met my Voice outside the Hostel. We recognised each other immediately.

He stood there at the side of the road, leaning against his bicycle. He appeared very beautiful to me. The depth of his soul, which I had sensed through his words, shone from his eyes, the hollows under his cheek bones were as subtly curved as weatherworn rocks. In the light of morning, we had lost the safety of the darkness and were both overcome by shyness. He asked me more than once where I had started from. Instead of telling him where

I lived in Cardiff, I had chattered on naively about our adventures on the mountain. I was very drawn to him, but we were going different ways and there seemed nothing I could do to change this. When we parted, I felt as if an elastic band was being stretched between my being and his. If it snapped it would be more than I could bear.

My friends must have found me rather silent as we hiked on that morning. I was reliving our last conversation in my mind. I realised that he had asked me more than once where I had started from. Naively, I had chattered on about our long walk. I had missed my chance of exchanging addresses. When we stopped for lunch I hardly tasted what I was eating. It was not until we had finished, that I put my hand into my rucksack for the block of chocolate he had given me as a parting gift. Chocolate always helped. I handed the block around.

"Something's tucked in the wrapping," said Gwenda, munching a square of the chocolate. She handed me a card.

I took it curiously. On the card was written clearly his precious address. He lived in the next town to me. I carried the card closely to me for the rest of the journey.

We did meet again, and it was the beginning of an important relationship. But that is another story.

13

MEMORY

SHE WAS SITTING at an iron table by the lake, in the park cafe, in the May sunshine. As I drew nearer to ask if I could sit in the empty seat next to her, I saw she had a carry-bag with books in it and an A4 notebook beside her. She lifted her head to indicate I could sit there, and I noticed she had been crying.

I said something about the weather.

She seemed glad enough to talk.

"I have been so looking forward to coming here to the park to do my revision." She shuffled the papers in front of her.

'You are a student, then?"

"Yes, I know I look too old to be a student, but I decided to return to study in my middle years, to read Psychology. This is my first year."

"Are you finding things interesting?" I asked automatically.

In my work as a counsellor, I spent time listening to people's problems: it had become part of my way of being. Something in my manner invited confidences. But I didn't really want to become involved in anyone's life at that moment. I had left my house to get away from the telephone, the unwashed dishes, the roses waiting to be cared for. The park was so restful. Here, gardening was done by someone else; a tray of tea and scones were made by someone else. I cut into a scone, and spread it with over-sweetened jam. I stirred the pot of tea, waiting for the tea bags to offer some colour.

"All year I've been writing essays and reading the recommended books. Since Christmas I've been working in my dingy room or in the library. I so looked forward to this fortnight, before the end of year exams, to sit here in the park to revise." A gust of wind lifted her hair, showing a stripe of grey over the ears. Out on the lake happy families in boats rowed and splashed.

"How is that going?"

Silent tears ran down her cheeks. Her features were intelligent, clear-cut.

"It took me by surprise. My memory isn't what it used to be. I was relying on it, and it has let me down. It's like a bereavement. In our studies we learn that age makes little difference to one's ability to remember things."

"Well, does it?" Seagulls swooped overhead. Their calls were loud, insistent. I noticed some cormorants high in the trees above us leaving their perch to dive for fish.

"I'm afraid it does make a difference. My memory used to work for me. Now it doesn't. It's like losing part of you. Like losing a limb."

The motorboat, taking people for a ride around the lake, bumped and splashed to a stop against the landing board. The engine was silent while passengers changed places, then it started chugging again.

"Perhaps your memory hasn't completely gone. Things will take longer to sink in, that's all."

"Maybe that's true. Revision will just take a lot longer. How I took my memory for granted! I thought I would be able to scan a page and remember what was on it like I used to. We think everything will last forever."

"I'm going to get you another coffee."

It was a year before I saw her again. There she was the following May, sitting at the same table by the lake, with books in front of her.

We greeted each other. " Remember me?" I said.

"You were good enough to listen to my problems."

"You were revising for exams. How did they go?

"I sort of managed. I worked late nights, remembered some facts with difficulty, and made things up as I went along. Practice did help to make my memory better."

"So long as you didn't give up."

"No, and I'm going on. But I'll be happy with a 2:2 instead of a 2:1 for my degree. Then I intend to work for a Masters.

"What subject will you focus on?"

"Memory," she said with a smile. "It deserves more research."

14

THE MIRROR

THERE WAS A leisurely atmosphere at the day hospital. We oldies sat around the tables on both sides of the room with offerings of tea and biscuits. What a blessing it was to be with people more or less of my own age. I had become used to being with much younger people. It was often a strain to keep up with them, to hear what they were saying, to try to remember the names of things and places when I was talking to them. Here, most people seemed to have trouble with remembering things, and were even less able. What a relief. I fell into a pleasant conversation with my neighbours, one on each side of the table. The usual round of blood tests, blood-pressure taking and form filling went on peaceably about us.

Our physio approached and we were rounded up for exercises. She led six of us to a pair of parallel bars by the opened windows. Rays of sunshine shone through the window, to fall on the polished wooden floor.

"You sense your position on the ground with your feet. Start with lifting your toes well up with each step, to avoid tripping. That will help towards dealing with falls. Now, to the count of fifteen..."

There we were, the six of us, the thin, the fat, the unsteady, each with a hand resting on the barre, carefully counting out our steps.

"That's very good. You'll feel stiff tomorrow, mind you. Now, one foot in front of the other, and see if you can manage without touching the barre. Just use it as a prop to support you if you need." We moved slowly along one side of the barre and turned around to come back. Why did I want to rise on my toes to turn. I looked up for a mirror.

Then it was with a white flash of memory I stepped back seventy years and I found the mirror. I was there in the mirror. I was back in Miss Marriot's studio in Charles Street, at my first ballet class.

"Stand up straight. Feet in first position, heels touching, well turned out," Miss Marriot was saying.

"When you swing your leg to the side, don't swing your bottom out," said our physio.

The instructions of Miss Marriott and our physio wove in and out of memory and merged together. As I stood there, I reheard many conversations that had taken place in the minutes, the hours, the days, the decades that had passed between then and now. I remembered the highlights from those early days to this as a drowning person is supposed to do, like a slide-show on the computer of my memory.

"Sit down and rest. You've worked hard to get this far."

How right she was. I have a pretty certificate on the piano at home to show my small success at ballet school.

There was no certificate on offer for today's work.

15

ON THE BEACH

IT WAS A grey day in late spring. We sat on the beach on knobbly pebbles, looking out over the horizon at the moving clouds, wondering if we should have our picnic lunch now, or risk the rain. There was a warm smell in the light wind, a damp salt-fishy smell.

A thin cry merged with the sound of swooping sea-birds. I looked towards the sea.

The stones were stepped in layers down to the grey sea, and surprisingly comfortable to sit on. We had levelled them out a bit, and covered them with our car blanket. We decided to delay lunch and went back to our books.

There were not many people about; most had decided it would rain.

I heard the distant call again. I looked up and saw a couple, small in the distance, coming over the curve of stones with an even smaller figure behind them. Behind them was the long line of sea and the small regular pulse of the waves. The sound was repeated, minimally louder.

"Mummy..."

And then the small voice was lost. But as the little creatures came slowly nearer, I heard it again.

"Mummy, I want to..."

The small voice had acquired urgency, but I still could not hear the words. The couple were slightly nearer. They did not stop or hesitate in their walk.

"Mummy, I want to do a pee."

At last I could make out the seriousness of this message. Yet her parents took it in their stride. At last there was an answering reply. "Hurry up Charlene, we'll be home soon."

"I can't wait until I'm home mummy. I want to do it now."

"Then do it in the sea Charlene. Go back and do it in the sea. We'll wait for you."

"I can't do it in the sea."

"Of course you can do it in the sea. You should have done it while we were down there. Now run back and take your pants down and do it there in the sea."

"I can't do it in the sea."

"Why can't you do it in the sea like everyone else?"

"I've just done it."

"How have you just done it Charlene?"

There was a long pause. The waves beat time patiently. There was a sad little cry in the wind. "I've done it in my knickers, mummy."

By now the distance between the three of them had closed. They were over the top of the pebbles and moving away from us, never to be seen or heard again.

16

SLOTTING IN THE SLAM

IF ANYONE WAS past competing in a Poetry Slam, it was me. I had spent the last week celebrating an advanced birthday, and the celebrations were fun - I'm not knocking them - but they don't make you feel any fitter. I wasn't sure where 'Ten Feet Tall' was, the silly name of the pub we were supposed to meet in. I would find it somehow.

I told myself, "It's a night out." And, "It's good practice." Good practice for what?

So there I was calling a taxi to I wasn't sure where. The taxi driver didn't have a clue where the pub was, but we knew it was near the Old Arcade, a popular pub of sacred memory. I was dropped off near the Castle - as near as you can get to Cardiff town these days, since the so-called improvements.

I had a bit of walking to do, and I'm getting breathless these days. I saw a group of lovely looking young men, and I asked them if they knew where the pub was. One of them brought out an amazing piece of technology, and entered 'Ten Feet Tall', the name of the wanted pub. In no time he reported the name of the street and exactly where it was. Technology is at an amazing stage, although it has advanced a bit too quickly for me. They turned out to be Greek students and we had a super conversation about the future of Greece: they showed me a picture on their latest piece of digital technology, of Stonehenge (I enjoyed the irony), where they had just visited. I would have been happy spending the evening with them, but I was programmed to take part in a Slam, wasn't I.

I got to the designated pub, and of course, the venue was up three flights of stairs. Take it very slowly, I told myself, and hope for the best. I carefully chose a double whisky at the bar and a bottle of ginger ale, my favourite standby, and found a seat. After a much needed rest, I asked in what order I was listed to read, and was told it was last. Good enough. I only hope I can stay awake that long. This reading order was important information - I knew I must pace the drinks to make them last. I do this in a very disciplined way, with a top-up. Next hurdle: it is very important to choose poems in the right order, if you want to win a poetry slam. I chose two reasonable ones to start, good enough to stay in the running but making sure to keep the best for later rounds if I was lucky enough to reach them. Fine judgements to be made! Our theme for the evening was 'Listening', because this evening was in aid of Samaritans. The money taken at the door was to go to them. I had spoken to one of the Samaritans who happened to be sitting near me, and I forged a close encounter with him in a short time, as you can do at poetry readings. He turned out to be one of the judges. The method is, each of the four judges write the score they choose on a sheet of paper and hold it up to be counted, as they do for ice-skating competitions.

I was a bit concerned to notice that the scorers started with rather high numbers, so there wasn't much room to go higher.

At last it was my turn to go into the lion's den. I had noticed that the stage was very high, but I imagined I would manage to climb up. In fact it was even higher than I had estimated; this stage that others were leaping onto was out of my league. In the end, I got up on it by turning on to my knees, as I have learned to do to get out of the bath. I announced that, "This is how I get out of the bath." There was applause. Then I approached the mike. It was much too high for me. "Another problem'" I said, but I detached the mike, and held it in my hand. By now, I guess the audience had got my measure: not very tall, and getting on a bit, but easy going.

I read a harmless poem to start with, about listening to the earth. My voice sounded a bit wibbly I thought. I followed this with a dramatic poem, about God not listening. When the numbers were held up to be read out, I heard a ten from my Samaritan, and someone else followed with a ten, so I was home and dry.

My Samaritan explained that the words of my poem so reflected his own feelings about how alone we are in the world, he connected with and appreciated what I had said.

The top six competitors went on to the second round. I read then the inimitable 'A Day in the Life of One Man and his Dog'. Who can beat that? It's funny, and people like a laugh. Soon I was into the final round - we were down to just the two of us competing for the final.

The other competitor was quite good, but his poems were not very lyrical. What was I to finish with? Someone advised a poem they had heard me read another evening. 'Over the Rainbow' - about a failed attempt to photograph a rainbow with an unpaid gas bill hanging over me, and that's what did it.

There were happy laughs of recognition - we've all got gas bills to pay and dreams that don't quite work out.

The prize was a much valued bottle of wine which I still have and look forward to drinking soon and just about enough money to cover what I had spent on taxis there and back, and the essential double whisky.

I have never felt that I so needed and deserved a prize. For unprecedented qualities of perseverance and survival.

And my poems are not bad.

17

ECLIPSE JUNKIE

MY OBSESSION WITH seeing the eclipse of the moon took me first to Verdun in Northern France, to stand under the Band of Totality, that narrow ribbon of sky around the earth where the eclipse is total. We drove from the ferry in good time for our adventure, but could not find a hotel for the night. We slept in the car as best we could. In the morning we waited for the clouds to clear. Just before the time of the eclipse the sky cleared, enough to see the strange atmospheric change of light and wind, but not enough to see clearly what was happening in the sky.

But something happened. The moon slowly covered the ancient sun, and the world changed. This was watched by waiting telescopes, cameras, and many pairs of eyes.

A strange quietness took over. The spirits of those who had died in that iconic war at Verdun, in the first world war, were present. They have always been there. We were standing in their place.

After this eclipse, as we walked away over the fields we came upon a sculpture by Rodin. It is a large sculpture in stone of an angel with lifted wings.

She is holding a dead soldier in her arms. She is an angel, but she looks at him with a mother's love, as if she will wrap him in her wings and take him to that heaven that I don't believe is up there.

But why is that stone carving alone in that field and not in a museum? Was it really there at all? I have searched for Rodin's work in the library. I haven't found it listed. But it was there that dawn morning, surrounded by the eternal spirits of Verdun. The souls of one of the dead soldiers was being lifted before my eyes and transported with love to a space in heaven that I experienced in those moments when the eclipsed sun was hidden behind the moon.

Four years later, I flew to Turkey to watch the eclipse of March 2005, with the Band of Totality overhead. The weather was very different from the previous eclipse experience in France: this time I was able to see it clearly. I chose a wild garden with palm trees, near a beach, to wait. The sandy beach was a short distance from the sea. Behind it, the sea swept in a wide arc. The vast stretch reminded me of Gwbert in West Wales. The horizon was long, long enough to show the curve of the world.

I settled on the grass in this haven under the sun, to watch and wait. I was surrounded by new friends. They possessed tripods, binoculars, telescopes: all the paraphernalia of astrophotography. I walked from one set-up to another, and joined in discussions about lenses, focal lengths, film choices and techniques. I had a small camera with me, but wisely decided to go for the visual experience, not the technical challenge: I was awed and impressed by those who owned and understood how to use the magic equipment. It was perfect theatre: a backdrop of paradise and a slow build-up under the sun, waiting for First Contact at noon. I relaxed under palm-tree shade, sipping wine. The grass was littered with small flowers, and the earth and the wine smelt sweet in the warm sunshine. The birds were busy and chatty in the low trees around us. I wondered what they would make of it.

At last a low hum rippled through the crowd.

"First Contact."

I had to look very hard through my dark glasses to see any change; then, on the moon's disc at the five o'clock position, was a tiny bite. It moved so slowly over the disc I had a sense of peace. There was no need to panic. But the birds did, and as the shape of the moon moved very slowly over the sun, they spoke to each other ever more excitedly. They moved in crowds from bush to small tree and back, chattering.

For a long time, the world looked the same. Although the moon is much smaller than the sun, because of its distance from us, in an eclipse it appears to cover the sun completely. But it will not do so forever. In a thousand or so years, the moon will have moved away from us and so will appear too small for this effect.

The sun was now a narrow crescent, shrinking almost imperceptibly. The last minutes had become quite cold. It was not completely dark, but the surrounding light became weird. All along the beach was a splendid sunset, not just around the setting sun, but along the entire skyline. Under this was a wide band of blue-green blending into a purple haze over the sea. The birds had decided to roost for the night. They thought the sun had set. Strange things were happening that I had been warned to look out for. Images of the crescent moon danced under the trees and between the long grasses. A nearby photographer called me over to see ripple formations on a white sheet, the 'shadow bars.' It was like the moving ripples on the bottom of a swimming pool.

Then I looked back to the sky. As the last narrowing of bright crescent closed up, there was a magic development of what seemed to be coloured beads along the edge.

"Bailey's Beads," someone said.

Then these were gone and there was left just one lovely disc that had been the moon. Now it was black, a velvety black, glowing darkly on a black sky, with only a minute edge of light trying to shine from behind its outer edges, the Corona.

The birds were silent.

Totality! There was a ripple of sound from the others.

Someone said, "You can look now without glasses."

We took off our glasses and we were able to look directly at the Corona. The eclipse of the sun was now total. I saw an incandescent halo of light glowing around our newly wedded sun and moon.

In this unfamiliar enchanted world of Totality I became aware of myself, of who I was, of what I had been doing with my life, where it was going, and the time I had left to live in it. I felt a renewed bond with our beloved earth, our place in it, and its place in the universe. I trusted our carbon damaged earth to mend itself, even if we have treated it so badly that it may not allow us to live here much longer.

I was aware of the awful events of the past: the wars, the injustices. The brutality and terrors that have been part of existence since the beginning of our life on earth.

At last, as the glowing discs moved apart, it was the end of Totality.

As the moon began to slip away from the sun, long rays emerged from prominences on one of the moon's edges: the Diamond Ring. The length and intensity of these rays vary for each eclipse according to the terrain on the exposed edge of the moon. This was a splendidly bumpy edge, so the rays were long and sparkling. Then there was the slow paced return of light as the two discs moved away from each other.

The sun was returned to us. I heard a round of applause from other watchers, and from the birds, who came out on the branches to have their say.

I look forward to seeing my next eclipse.

18

YOU'RE GOING TO BE -

"THE FLAT HAS long been taken," the soft-voiced Indian woman told her. "I have let it to a student who is going to start college in January. But you may rent it for a few months, until then."

Looking over the flat was only a token gesture. There were not many choices if you were homeless and had a small child to care for. She had left her husband and her home and did not want to stay with disapproving members of her family.

The kitchen opened onto a paved yard. She observed that the yard would be useful for her six year old son, Peter.

"The yard," the landlady warned her, "is shared by the students. Now they are very nice girls, but they are young and have many parties. The neighbours grumble a good deal. Also, late nights are not good for their health. You look a sensible girl. I wonder if you would say that you have orders from me to stop parties after twelve o'clock."

She did not say it then, but she had no intention of playing the part of matron, because she did not feel it. She heard music and chatter coming from a room upstairs, and she longed to be part of it.

The neighbourhood was lively. Next door was a betting shop, and she could hear information over the speaker from first thing in the morning until ten at night. On Saturdays and big race days the street was parked with cars two deep. Children played in and out of the doorways.

The front door bell rang a good deal. Often she ran to open it; she did not expect it would be for her, but she was the nearest. More than once, she let in a shy quiet boy. She noticed his downward sloping eyes, under a hood of frizzy hair, and his pale face. Always, he carried a music case; she could not guess what instrument rested in the curves. He would disappear upstairs. He never stayed long. She could hear his steps treading slowly down, minutes later.

Her own life was on hold until the children's officer had made his call. He was to prepare a report to be read in court for the custody of their son. The report would assess if she was a fit mother. She felt anxious about this visit. She was the one after all who had left the family house, and legal implications followed. She did not know what day or what time he would call, so she wore what she considered to be her 'good mother' outfit each day.

When at last she opened the door to the children's officer, she had a moment to reflect that Peter was no grubbier than his usual end of school-day self, and that she hadn't been heard to shout, or to smack him.

This was an exam she must not fail. "Do come in, and have some tea."

"No tea thank you, I had a cup on my last call."

"Well I need some, if you don't."

She disappeared into the kitchen to take several deep breaths, and make one cup of strong tea, with extra sugar. That was it. He'd know now that she was too neurotic to be a good mother. She had the odd feeling that it had all happened before. The white tiles of the kitchen blurred into the tiles of the hospital where she'd had Peter. There was some doubt then whether she would manage the birth without assistance. Now it seemed that she had proved inadequate to the task. By a time reversal, the pain of birth, the six years of days and nights of caring, the teething, the feeding, would be relived, and yet the child disappear into a womb-like darkness as if he had never been.

The interview was simple enough. He went through the form filling, starting with name, address and age, while her voice grew stronger. Then he went on to more difficult questions. She drew Peter into the yard to play

with his bicycle. Then, it was easy to talk to this reasonable and kindly person. Once more her motherhood became an immutable fact.

When all the forms were filled, he put away the papers, and leaned back. "Now I would judge that you have
no reason to worry, and you will be hearing from us
shortly. But I would like to say that you are going to be
very lonely, you know."

After he had gone, the tensions of the visit left her
feeling restless and depressed. His last words, and the
way that he had said them, repeated over and over in her
head. She did her face, put on a cool dress, and went out
to join Peter.

The flat had been darkened by the drawn curtains
and her thoughts. Coming out into the yard was like
coming back into the world. The sun fell hotly on the
dusty earth; now the students were returning, the barren
ground was transformed into an oasis by their coloured
dresses and shirts. Some were sitting in deck-chairs, some
were sprawled on makeshift benches of planks and bricks
that littered the space.

Peter was feeding his tortoise. It was the one pet they
could manage in the circumstances. "Man's gone," she
said. He didn't answer. He was offering the tortoise some
clover.

One of the girls, a tall one she had heard someone
call 'Valerie', looked up. "I wonder if I could ask you

a favour," she asked quietly. "When Fred calls next, would you say I'm not in?"

"You mean the boy with the frizzy hair? What's the matter? Don't you like him?"

"Not all that much. It would be possible if he were taller. I feel bad enough being the height I am. With him, I feel terrible."

"Well, I'm shorter than you in every way. You can send him down to me if you like."

It was simpler, after that, not to answer the door. In that long hour after her son was asleep, the walls of the room closed in and became the limits of her world. In that reduced space, memories and regrets were compressed to their essence.

She had felt lonely before, in her single days. But then she had been free to come and go as she pleased. She could call on friends, have a meal out, go for a walk. But now, she could not do these simple things. In the evenings, she was chained to these rooms by the need of her sleeping child as surely as a prisoner in a cell. As it was, she often let him stay up later than was good for him, to shorten the evening. At bedtime, he needed to talk about his father. Although it was painful, she could not refuse him. Now at last he was asleep. There was only the washing up of plates, the dark floor to look at, and the shrinking walls. She wondered how soon she could go to bed without the risk of waking too early next morning.

She jumped at the sound of a knock. There were two shadows on the glass door to her flat. She opened it to Valerie and Fred. "Come in," she said.

"Well, I can't stay," said Valerie, "but Fred can." She introduced them and was gone.

"Coffee for two, then," she said. Fred was silent. He was not beautiful, but he had a glow of youth, and his features were sharp and delicate.

"You like her, but there's another boy or something?"

"Or something. Yes, I do rather. But I don't let it get me down. There are other women in the world."

He told her about himself. It seemed he was almost half her age. For some reason, that pleased them both. He was studying music at the local college, classical music, but for himself he composed and played jazz. He spoke with a slight stutter that was converted into thoughtful pauses. She gave him a potted history of herself. As they spoke, sitting on cushions in front of the gas fire, with Peter asleep in the bedroom, the rest of world receded.

He left at midnight, giving her a brief kiss. He was going for a walk across the park. That was where, he said, he worked out his music themes, and practised playing his trumpet in the dark, under the trees, away from neighbours.

She fell asleep easily that night, and didn't think about Fred.

The next evening, she opened the door to him.

"Valerie may be in."

"I've come to see you."

"Great."

That evening, Fred didn't hesitate so much. He seemed even younger, quite light-hearted. She too was at ease. He wasn't a power-fuelled dream-boat. He wasn't marriageable, he was just a friend. After Peter had fallen asleep and they had finished the spaghetti bolognese they had made together, the feel of his arms around her waist was reassuring. Loose ends knitted together. "Now what," she thought. Fred touched her body with lingering delicacy, as if she was too precious to hurry. He was twenty-four years old. This was the lovemaking she remembered at seventeen, and she had not outgrown it. Life was worth living.

"Don't send me home tonight. My place is cold and dreary."

"Oh, might as well stay." There were two beds in the bedroom. "Just sleep then."

"Yes."

"I've been sharing with Peter. Heaven knows what harm it's doing him, but we've sort of just got into it. There are two beds. You can have the spare one."

Peter woke up as he often did, and called out to her in the dark. "I'm coming now," she said, undressed quickly, and snuggled up to him. How small his body seemed. He put his arms around her sleepily. "Fred's staying the night," she said. "He's sleeping over there in the other bed." Peter became bright and chatty for a while. Then he got vaguer, and soon she heard him breathing more deeply.

There was a rustling of covers being thrown back, and soft footfalls on the floor boards, coming nearer. Then Fred climbed in beside her.

She was enveloped. The bed sagged in the middle, warm bodies enclosed each side, and the blankets covered closely. One of Peter's arms lay across her chest. He was deeply asleep; his appley breath fell regularly on her cheek. Fred's arm lay around her waist, and she could feel his warmth from shoulder to foot.

A pocket of warmth enclosed her. She did not know where her body began and where it ended, and where each body that loved her, or wanted love, began or ended.

She could hear the echo of the social worker's words - "You're going to be" - then the words eluded her. The echo faded. She felt safe. Tomorrow was an eternity of friendly night away.

They were survivors in a life-boat. They were protected from the elements. Through a crack in the canvas sheet, she could see the moon and sky, but there was no wind. They had slipped their moorings. As far as the eye could see, rocky daytimes jutted harshly, but the boat navigated a channel of velvety water through the blankety dark.

19

MID-LIFE CRISIS

I WAS RUNNING A small craft shop at the time, selling my own stuff. It was early spring, but I didn't feel good about it. The shop was rather quiet, time to take stock. As well as feeling depressed, I had lost my drive to create anything any more. This state could last forever. What could life now hold? Empty hours had been illuminated by painting and sculpture: dramatic happenings had been transformed into writing. That was gone. What was the point of life now?

In the middle of this mid-life crisis, a student entered the shop with a pile of books under his arm. He put them down on the counter and began to look at the goods on sale. I looked at the books.

He said, "You can have them if you like. I don't want them any more. No use to me."

"What's wrong with them?"

"It's me. I don't want to study any more. I've done one year, but the subject's not for me."

"You mean that you've been studying psychology and you don't find it interesting. I can't believe it."

"Well, if you want them, they are yours."

"What will you do?"

"Off to the army maybe. I'll have a few drinks first." His words were slightly blurred. He combed his hand through unwashed hair, gave the books a parting tap, and ambled out.

The idea that anyone with an opportunity to study this subject could turn their back on it amazed me. I would be so happy to be studying it. In a moment of realisation, I wished that I was in a position to do so. The creative drive had dropped out of my life, but my brain seemed to be as before, and underused. Other people had degrees, where was mine?

I rang up the university to enquire about entry forms. A pleasant voice answered, "Next week is interviewing week. To avoid delay, why not make an appointment now?"

My preparation for the interview was to have a good read of the books that had been left on the counter. Then I listed the titles and the authors' names, and learned the list.

At the interview, I was asked what books I had read on my subject. So I repeated my learned list. I remember that the tutor then asked me what facet of human nature especially interested me. I have long been intrigued by the Milgram experiment, where participants are told by someone in author-ity to give electric shocks to others hidden behind a screen. The surprise is that so many agree to carry out such orders. Only a few were able to resist. We had a pleasant discussion.

An I.Q. test followed that we were assured was only for students to practise giving tests, and I was in.

So I, a mature student of fifty something, joined a handful of other mature students of thirty something, and the regular students, for a three year degree course in social psychology at Cardiff University, starting that September. I had no time to ponder on my mid-life crisis, and I am not sure where it has gone.

20

MY TWO AUNTS

I REMEMBER THE SHINY patent shoes I had when I was six. They fastened with a strap in front of my ankle. They were silent on the stair carpet, but when I reached the tiled hall, they made a satisfying clippity-clop. My aunts were waiting for me by the open door. We were going for a walk to the shops. My Aunt Rae took my hand and we went out into in the spring sunshine.

We paused. A large earthworm was moving across the pavement. I noted him carefully. He was a very wormy worm, with clearly marked circles and a bluish stain about his middle. He was sloping at a steady pace towards the hedge.

My Aunt Rae said, "Now whatever you do Betty, don't step on that worm."

Step on it? What an extraordinary thing to suggest. But I supposed you could. I heard the last words again, "Step on that worm."

So I lifted one of my shiny black shoes and brought the heel down on the poor worm in one step. It felt firm a first, then gave way easily.

My Aunt Rae made a strange sound. I looked at her and saw her jaw had dropped, making her mouth a small dark hole.

"But that is exactly what I told the child not to do," she said to Aunt Anne. How could she do such a thing?"

"Yes, I heard you tell her not to. And that is exactly what she has done."

It was the same with the red berries on the bush along the street. I was told not to eat them: I did, and I got an awful stomach-ache . But I survived, which is more than can be said for the worm.

We were a close family. My two aunts were a part of my growing up. I related to each one in a different way. Aunt Rae was small and precise. I loved to watch her packing parcels. She used real brown paper of course, shiny side out. She managed to cut the paper into exactly the right size for the enclosure. She carefully folded and tucked in the raw edge. Then the envelope ends would be folded exactly, and the new folds flattened with her well cared for buffed fingers. With unfailing regularity, she packed and sent cigarettes to her brother in hospital, shell-shocked since the first world war. As a child, I was often sent to buy the cigarettes: she didn't know that I hated this task because the local shopkeeper thought I was buying them for myself, and I couldn't explain who they were for because of the unspoken shame that hung over his illness.

Aunt Anne was taller and more street-wise. She was always well groomed. She polished her quality leather handbags, and the soles of her shoes as well as the tops. She was a business woman, successful, self-made.

When the sisters were growing up together, the smaller of the two, Aunt Rae, was the dominant one. As fate would have it, it was the dominant one who became ill, with slow-moving but inexorable Parkinson's disease. Because of the ravages of the first world war, and the natural diffidence of both sisters, neither of them managed to settle with a partner. And so it fell to the tall, sensitive Anne to be the carer.

I was invited to join them for lunch in town one Saturday. While the waiter stood with notebook poised, Aunt Rae kept us waiting for her deliberation. Would the fish be cooked enough? Would it have bones? Would it be fresh? Conversation waited. When our meal arrived, and hers had been carefully tested, conversation was more or less resumed. I gradually realised that she was queen. It was her health, her wishes, her ego, that ruled the day.

My Aunt Anne had survived the buzz bombs of the war, daring to stay in London to build her business during those dark days. She wasn't afraid of the bombs. But now, when Aunt Rae said, "Time to go," Anne stopped in the middle of a sentence, to do as she was told, and we left.

When my aunts retired and left London, they bought a house together in Cardiff, to be near the rest of the family. I visited often, but not as often as I felt I should.

They made rules of space and time, to try to make it easier for them to live together. Rae was to go to the bedroom to rest in the afternoons. Anne was to be allowed to read the daily paper without interruption after the evening meal. But the rules weren't always adhered to, and the rows that followed were bitter. Recriminations were dragged up from a distant and unhappy past that I only dimly knew about. My sympathies were for Anne, but I didn't know how to help. She was trapped. I too felt caught up in the cycle of guilt and regret.

In the end, old people's homes were tried and found to be unsatisfactory in varying degrees, but inevitable. Death, when it came, seemed merciful, first for Rae with her illness, then years later, for Anne.

I mourned them both, honed my guilt, and resolved to die independent, and when the time came, if possible, without too much delay.

21

CHARLIE SEAGULL

W E CALLED HIM Charlie, but it was no proper name for this spectacular seagull that appeared out of the blue to befriend us. We could have called him Jonathan perhaps, after the iconic Jonathan Seagull of the cult novel I remember reading in my teens.

He literally appeared out of the blue. Eric and I were sitting about in our small garden, glad of the late sunshine. It was a quiet weekend; no one called. Even the sky was empty, except for some small high clouds. There was a buzz, and as we looked up two planes crossed the sky, leaving their vapour trails. The trails soon faded, and the sky was empty again. Then we noticed a bird circling overhead. He started from so high we could hardly see what it was, then he descended in smaller circles to come to rest on the telegraph pole we are lucky enough to have at the bottom of the garden, with clearly marked black feathers in a pattern we got to know so well. Sitting on the top of that pole, a bird could surely detect the noises made by incoming telephone messages.

I know so little about the sentient life of birds, what they see and hear, what the world means to them. He looked at us from this vantage point, seemed to decide we were friendly, and flew nearer to land on the flat roof of our neighbour's house. Here he rested in the sunshine and stared at us. First he looked at us from on eye with his head at an angle, and then he turned to face us and looked again. And he took in the dish of cat-food on the garden table.

He walked up and down on the roof-top, staring downward. We could only see the top part of his body moving. He spread his wings and descended to the stones on the garden wall, then to the table-top, to eat the cat-food. As he ate, he turned sideways and his formidable beak clacked against the metal dish with every mouthful. After every few gulps, he washed it down with water from a bowl near-by, and when he had finished, he dipped his head into the bowl and shook it briskly once or twice, to clean his beak.

When the food was eaten, he looked at us again. I hurried indoors to open another tin of cat-food, with a sense of accurate communication at a primitive level. This was an alien being, but we understood each other.

After that first meeting, Charlie visited often. I noticed that once he had perched on his chosen place, he would made loud gull sounds. I don't know what the sounds meant, but I noticed their result. All other gulls that had been flying in the vicinity hurried away, screeching loudly.

He calls to see us about three times a day. Usually after eating, he dips his head into his bowl, and shakes it briskly to spray off the water. Sometimes when the sun is hot, he steps inside the bowl and lowers his whole body into the water. When he turns to go, the sun shines through his outer tail feathers, making them translucent.

Sometimes he calls by, yet ignores the food we set out. He will just sit on the flat roof in the sunshine, resting and looking at us, sometimes with one eye, sometimes with two. We were concerned for him when this first happened. Was he ill? Did he want different food? Gradually, I sensed that he calls to visit us even when he isn't hungry, because we mean the same to him as he means to us.

After his hard day flying and fighting, he is as glad to stop by and sit near us for friendly companionship, as we are to have him near.

He has become a welcome friend in a hard and uncaring world.